The
Blue Tit Travels
Africa

To my Blue Eyed Boy,
it's all for you.

The Little Blue Tit was feeling fed up.

The swallows had been talking about their adventures again.

Blue tits didn't go on adventures.

The other blue tits kept telling him so.

"We are not the sort of birds
that do that.

All that doing and doing quickly,
meeting different scary animals
isn't a good thing at all!"
they would say.

But the Little Blue Tit wanted to be the sort of bird that
did do things, he wasn't scared of
animals that were different from him.

"If the swallows can go on adventures
then so can I!" the Little Blue Tit thought.

So off the Little Blue Tit flew...

The first animal he met after flying for a very long time was...

an elephant.

"Whoah!" he said,
"you've got really big teeth!
Is that your nose?! Are you really old? You have
wrinkly skin!" said the cheeky Little Blue Tit.

The elephant
laughed
a deep,
slow
laugh.

"Well, they're not called
my teeth," said
the elephant gently,
"they're called my tusks.
This is my trunk and I am
old compared to you,
my little friend."

"I've never seen an animal like you before, you're so different!" said the Little Blue Tit.

"And so are you to me," the elephant said.

Hmmmm thought the Little Blue Tit.
"Different isn't scary at all!
I wonder who I will meet next?"

The next animal he met was... a zebra.

"Hello, where have you come from?"
asked the zebra.

"I've flown all the way from England and I'm
having an adventure, what are you?"

"I'm a zebra, you can
tell by my bold stripes,"
explained the
proud zebra.

"You are so beautiful,"
said the Little Blue Tit
in wonder.

"Thank You,"
replied the zebra,
"and you are very pretty."

The Little Blue Tit blushed.
"I've never seen an
animal like you before,
you're so different,"
said the Little Blue Tit.

Hmmmm thought
 the Little Blue Tit.

"Different isn't scary,

I wonder who
 I will meet next?"

The next animal he met was... a giraffe.

The Little Blue Tit was flying and singing, when he saw a very tall tree with a very tall animal next to it, chewing a mouthful of leaves.

"Nom, nom, nom," said the big friendly face as the Little Blue Tit landed next to him.

"Hello, you are very tall! What are you?" asked the Little Blue Tit.

"Nom, munch, crunch, I can reach the best, juiciest leaves up here. Nom, crunch, munch. I'm a giraffe, nom, was that you singing? Chew, crunch," asked the giraffe.

"Oh yes I love to sing, don't you?" replied
the Little Blue Tit. The giraffe grinned,
"Nooo I don't sing, but your singing was lovely."

"Thank-you,"
said the Little Blue Tit
leaving the giraffe to his dinner.
Hmmmm thought
the Little Blue Tit.

"Different isn't scary, I wonder
who I will meet next?"

a rhinoceros.

The next animal he met was...

"Look at you!" said the Little Blue Tit.
"You have horns!"

The Little Blue Tit was looking into the face of an
awesome white rhino.

"Phuumfph," exhaled the rhino. "Who are you?"
he asked in a deep gruff voice.

"I'm a blue tit" said the Little Blue Tit. "Are you
a chubby unicorn?!"

The Rhino laughed, "No, I'm a rhinoceros but
my friends call me Rhino."

"A rhinofothus?" asked the Little Blue Tit.

"Almost," chuckled the rhinoceros,
"but you can call me Rhino."

"Thank you Rhino, it's nice to meet you! I've never
met an animal like you before, you're so different!"
said the Little Blue Tit happily.

Hmmmm thought the Little Blue Tit.

"Different isn't scary,
I wonder who I will meet next?"

The next animal he met was... **a lion.**

"Wow look at you! You're really fluffy."

Yawning the lion said, "Oh, I don't want to talk right now,
I've just eaten my dinner and I'm so very sleepy."

"Are you a big fluff puff cat?" asked the Little Blue Tit.

The lion grinned. "Ahh, nooo. I am a lion,"
He said as he looked at him through sleepy eyes.
"Fluff Puff..." he muttered with a grin,
stretching his big paws.

"I think I'll leave you to sleep," decided
the Little Blue Tit.

Hmmmm thought the Little Blue Tit.

"Different isn't scary,
I wonder who I will meet next?"

The next animal he met was...

a hippopotamus.

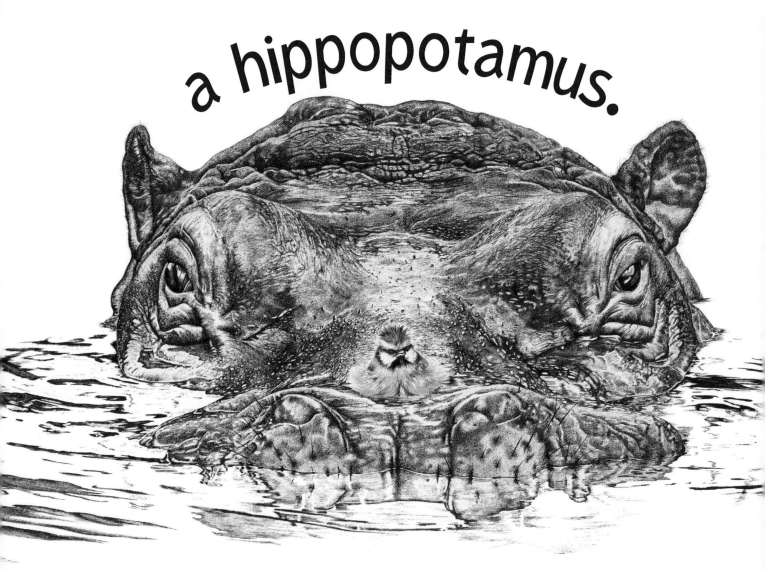

The Little Blue Tit came to a river where he saw some
very big animals splashing and playing.

"Hello there!" said the Little Blue Tit.

"Blub, blubble lub, pop! hello there," said the big animal as he blew bubbles in the water.

"Is it bathtime? That looks like fun! Can I play too?" asked the Little Blue Tit excitedly.

"Of course you can!" said the big animal.

"What are you?" asked the Little Blue Tit.
"Are you a really big fish?"

"I'm a hippopotamus, hippo for short" he said with a smile.
"I think I'll call you a hippo as I don't think I can say hiplodotamus easily," giggled the Little Blue Tit.

"You may be right, pop, bubble lop,"
laughed the hippo.

"I've never met an animal like you before,
you're so different!"

Hmmmm thought the Little Blue Tit.

"Different isn't scary.

I wonder who I will meet next?"

Feeling tired the Little Blue Tit decided to rest.

Finding a cosy, fluffy bush,
the Little Blue Tit settled down and slept.

"Good Morning," said a deep voice.

"Morning," yawned the Little Blue Tit.

The Little Blue Tit realised it wasn't a fluffy bush he'd slept in but a

very
large,
grey,
fluffy
animal.

"Oh," he said, "who are you?"
"I am a gorilla
and you landed on my shoulder last night.
Did you sleep well?" asked the gorilla.

"Oh yes I did, thank you! I've been on an adventure and I've met many different animals," said the Little Blue Tit proudly.

"Were you scared?" asked the gorilla.

"No, different isn't scary. It's just different."

"Yes, different is not scary," agreed the gorilla.

"Where will you go to
next Little Blue Tit?"
asked the gorilla.

The Little Blue Tit
thought...

Hmmmmm.

Now where shall I go to next?

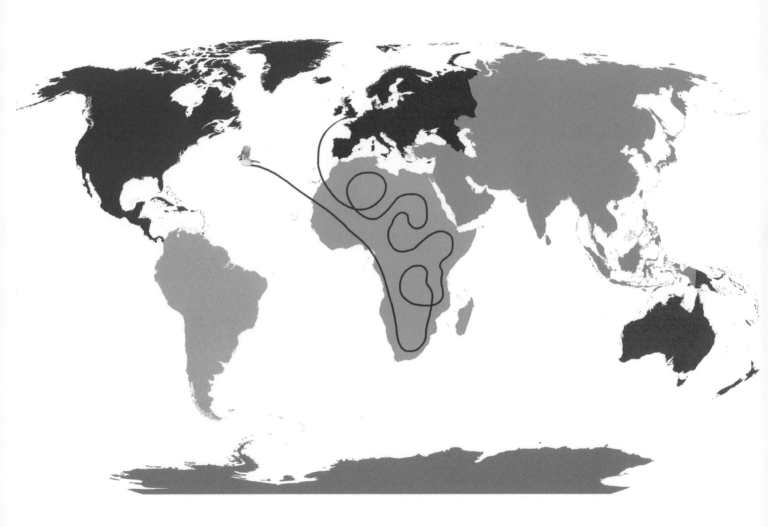

Join the Little Blue Tit on his next
adventure to North America -
coming soon.

Here you can draw who you would like
the Little Blue Tit to meet next! It can be an
animal or even someone you know.

Did you know that ALL the animals
the Blue Tit met on his adventure
are endangered?

Some are even critically endangered
and they really need help.

It is sad to understand so many
beautiful animals are
endangered or vulnerable.

Can you help?

Yes you can!

There are many charities that are
helping to protect these
endangered animals.

Take a look at:

www.explorersagainstextinction.com

About the Author

Astra is an artist and children's book
author based in Suffolk, England.
She has one son (all grown up)
and a cat called Dave.

Astra annually donates art to the
conservation charity
Explorers Against Extinction.

This amazing charity helps protect the
beautiful animals she loves to draw.

www.astraoriginalartworks.com

astra_original_art

All illustrations are Astra's original pen drawings.

Astra's new children's book is now available.

Bee Bums
and the
Bums of Bees!

Have you seen a bee's bum?
A busy, tizzy, whizzy bum...

Join in the fun of
The Busy Bee Bum Hum!

Lots of bees means lots of bums!

Bee Bums
and the
Bums of Bees!

Written and illustrated
by
Astra

Printed in Great Britain
by Amazon

86840417R00022